D0577469

# That's Philomena!

by Catherine Bancroft and Hannah Coale

pictures by Hannah Coale

FROG BEAUTIFUL

Simon & Schuster Books for Young Readers

SIMON & SCHUSTER BOOKS FOR YOUNG READERS
An imprint of Simon & Schuster Children's Publishing Division
1230 Avenue of the Americas
New York, NY 10020
Text copyright © 1995 by Catherine Bancroft and Hannah Coale
Illustrations copyright © 1995 by Hannah Coale
All rights reserved including the right of reproduction
in whole or in part in any form.
SIMON & SCHUSTER BOOKS FOR YOUNG READERS
is a trademark of Simon & Schuster.
Designed by Christy Hale
The text of this book is set in Egyptian Light.
The illustrations are rendered in watercolors.
Manufactured in the United States of America
10  9  8  7  6  5  4  3  2  1
Library of Congress Cataloging-in-Publication Data
Bancroft, Catherine.
That's Philomena! / Catherine Bancroft and Hannah Coale. — 1st ed.
p.    cm.
Summary: When Philomena hears her brothers and sisters calling her
"Philomeany," she devises a plan to make them realize that she is a
nice big sister after all.
[1. Frogs—Fiction.]   2.Behavior—Fiction.    3. Brothers and sisters—Fiction.]
I. Coale, Hannah.    II. Title.    III. Title : That is Philomena.
PZ7.B2177Th   1995
[E]—dc20   94-8017
ISBN:0-02-708326-8

For my beloved siblings, who saw me
through this story both in life and art
— H.C.

For Jane and Alice and Luke
— C.B.

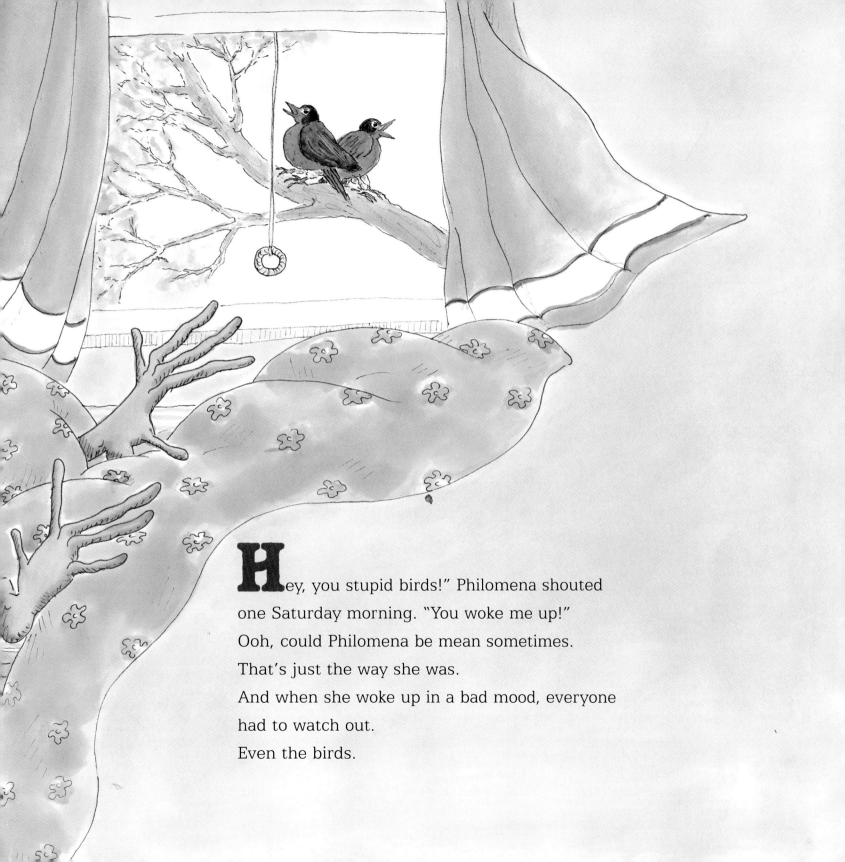

**H**ey, you stupid birds!" Philomena shouted
one Saturday morning. "You woke me up!"
Ooh, could Philomena be mean sometimes.
That's just the way she was.
And when she woke up in a bad mood, everyone
had to watch out.
Even the birds.

Philomena pushed her door open and spied her little
brother, Felix. "Can't you build your castles someplace
else?" she grumped, and she sent his tower flying.

"And, Freda, do you have to carry that gross old bear everywhere you go?" Philomena snapped. "It doesn't even have eyes." Then she glared at Phoebe. "I think it's time you gave up that bottle," she said with a sniff.

Philomena's brother Frank was in the bathroom. "Does it take twenty hours to brush your teeth?" Philomena shouted through the door. "Wow," said Frank. "You're in a great mood." Philomena flounced into the bathroom and banged the door shut.

Now, Philomena's brothers and sisters had a secret
name for her. And it just so happened that this morning
Philomena heard it by mistake.

"Uh-oh," whispered Frank as Philomena sailed in to breakfast.

"Here comes Philo**meany**."

"Yeah, here comes Philo**meany**," whispered Felix.

"Here comes Philo**meany**," Freda whispered to her bear.

Phoebe banged her spoon on the table.

Philomena's mouth dropped open. She couldn't believe her ears.

"Now, kids," said Daddy Frog. "That's enough."
He folded up his paper. "Frank, Phoebe, it's time to
go to the store."
"Have a nice breakfast, Philomena," Mommy Frog said.
"I'm off to weed the garden."
"Me and Freda are coming, too, Mommy," said Felix.

Philomena was all alone. She sat down at the table and poured some cereal. But Philomena couldn't eat. Her stomach hurt.

"How could they call me that horrible name?" she whispered to the birds on the windowsill. The birds just flew away.

Philomena turned on the
water and rinsed her bowl.
"Don't they know what a nice
big sister I can be?" she said.
"*Phhhhilomeany,*" said the faucet.

"Even if I'm cranky sometimes,
that's not exactly mean!" she
said. She slammed her bowl
into the dishwasher and pushed
the button.
"*ShhhPhilomeany, shhhPhilomeany,*"
said the dishwasher.
"Stop that!" she shouted, kicking
the dishwasher.

"Ouch!"

Philomena limped to the table and sat down. "All right," she muttered. "I'm just going to have to show them how wrong they are. I'm just going to have to do something so nice, they're going to regret the day they ever called me that name!" She grabbed a pad of paper.

"Okay," she said. "What can I do?"

BUY TOYS FOR EVERY SINGLE ONE OF MY BROTHERS AND SISTERS, she wrote. "Forget it," she said. "That would use up all my allowance."

CLEAN EVERYONE'S ROOM. "Nah," she said. "Too hard." She chewed on the end of her pencil. "I know!" she said. MAKE YUMMY BROWNIES. "I'd like to see them call me *Philomeany*, now!" She jumped up and went to work.

Philomena had just found some baking chocolate when
the screen door banged open. "Hey, Philomena." It was
Felix and Freda. "Will you come and help us?"

"No," said Philomena. "I'm busy."

"Oh, come on, Philomena. We want to make a lemonade stand.

We want it to be a real store. Please."

"Oh, all right." Philomena sighed, and she followed them outside.

"I can't believe you want me to build a lemonade stand with this junky old wood," Philomena said. But she did it, anyway.

"Felix," Philomena ordered, "hand me my tools. Freda, you're in charge of nails. And don't anybody make any noise. I'm concentrating." Philomena worked furiously.

"Wow," said Freda when it was all done.

"Gosh, it's beautiful," said Felix.

"I know," said Philomena. "Now don't bother me anymore."

And she headed back to the kitchen.

"Okay. Brownies," Philomena said. She scanned the recipe. "No problem. Anyone can do this." She found all the stuff she needed.

I really am an incredibly nice big sister, Philomena thought, beating the eggs. She turned on the radio. "Wonderful *Philonicey*," she sang. There was a sound at the door.

Felix and Freda had their faces pressed against the screen.
"Philomena! We gotta have a sign!" Felix said. "It needs to say
LEMONADE 10 CENTS, and I don't know how to spell lemonade
and Freda doesn't, either."
Philomena wiped her hands. "Will you guys stop bothering
me!" she grumped. But she found some cardboard, anyway,
and some markers.

Philomena made really big letters, and Felix and Freda colored them in.

Philomena went back to the
kitchen. "Now, where was I?"
She poured the batter into a pan
and stuck it in the oven.
"There," she said. "A masterpiece!"

"Philomena! We forgot the
most important thing!"
Philomena stomped to the door.
"What is it now?"
"Lemonade, Philomena! You
can't have a lemonade stand
without lemonade!" Felix yelled.

"Everybody knows that!"
Philomena snorted. She went
to the freezer. She mixed up
a huge batch of lemonade and
cut up lemons for the top.

She carried it out to the stand with
the ice cubes bumping against the jug.
"Hey, knuckleheads," she said. "Your
sign is upside down!"
And she fixed it.

When Philomena got back to the kitchen, smoke was billowing from the oven. "Oh, no!" she screamed. "My brownies!" Philomena's brownies were burned to a crisp.

"I'll never be *Philonicey*, now!" cried Philomena, slumping into her chair. She put her head on the table and sobbed. "My goodness, dear, what's wrong?" said Mommy Frog as she came in from the garden.

"Oh, Mommy," Philomena moaned. "I **was** mean this morning. And now the brownies I baked came out horrible. They're right. I am *Philomeany!*"

"I see," said her mother. She gave Philomena a hug. Philomena rubbed her nose. Then she sighed. "I guess I know what I have to do," she said. "And it's gross."

Philomena stomped across the grass to the lemonade stand.
Everyone was there.

"First of all, I have something to say," she announced,
glaring at her brothers and sisters. "I don't want you to call
me *Philomeany* anymore. I hate it. That's number one. And
number two: I know I was a stinky, mean big sister this
morning, so I tried to make some brownies for you guys,
but I wrecked them. Anyway, I'm sorry. So there."

Frank's mouth fell open. "Wow," he said. "Amazing.
You apologized."
Philomena glowered at him. "Yeah, well, don't get
too used to it."

"Hold on, you guys," said Daddy Frog. "Will someone please
tell me where this lemonade stand came from?"

"Philomena made it," Felix explained.

"I was in charge of nails," said Freda proudly.

"I gotta admit, Philomena," Frank said, "when you're not
being a pain, you really can be kind of amazing."

"I can?" said Philomena. She smiled a big smile.

Mommy Frog winked at Philomena. "You've had a very
busy day," she said. "I think it's time for some lemonade."

So everybody sat in the grass. Freda gave out cups and
Felix poured lemonade.
Philomena lay back and gazed at the sky. "You know,"
she said. "Since you guys won't be calling me *Philomeany*
anymore, I have an idea."
"Uh-oh," said Frank.

"What do you think of *Philamazing*?" she asked.

"Oh, gross," said Frank. "Let's get her."

And they did.

V9-BZX-442

Cascade Library
505 S. Highland Dr.
Kennewick, WA 99337

Discard

R.L. 3.9
0.5

Discard

# SAVING
## Sweetness

**DIANE STANLEY**

ILLUSTRATED BY

**G. BRIAN KARAS**

Cascade Library
505 S. Highland Dr.
Kennewick, WA 99337

## G. P. PUTNAM'S SONS
### NEW YORK

Text copyright © 1996 by Diane Stanley
Illustrations copyright © 1996 by G. Brian Karas
All rights reserved. This book, or parts thereof, may not be reproduced
in any form without permission in writing from the publisher.
G. P. Putnam's Sons, a division of The Putnam & Grosset Group,
200 Madison Avenue, New York, NY 10016.
G. P. Putnam's Sons, Reg. U.S. Pat. & Tm. Off.
Published simultaneously in Canada.
Printed in Hong Kong by South China Printing Co. (1988) Ltd.
Design by Cecilia Yung and Donna Mark
Text set in Else Semibold.
The illustrations were done in gouache, acrylic and
pencil with toned cyanotype photographs.

Library of Congress Cataloging-in-Publication Data
Stanley, Diane. Saving Sweetness / by Diane Stanley;
illustrated by G. Brian Karas.  p.  cm.
Summary: The sheriff of a dusty western town rescues Sweetness,
an unusually resourceful orphan, from nasty old
Mrs. Sump and her terrible orphanage.
[1. Orphans—Fiction. 2. West (U.S.)—Fiction.
3. Humorous stories.] I. Karas, G. Brian, ill. II. Title.
PZ7.S7869Sav  1996  [E]—dc20  95-10621 CIP AC
ISBN 0-399-22645-1
5  7  9  10  8  6  4

*For Dad and Claire, a warm Texas howdy* –D.S.

*For JJ and David, Scott and Ava* –G.B.K.

Out in the hottest, dustiest part of town is an orphanage run by a female person nasty enough to scare night into day. She goes by the name of Mrs. Sump, though I doubt there ever was a Mr. Sump on accounta she looks like somethin' the cat drug in and the dog wouldn't eat. I heard that Mrs. Sump doesn't much like seein' the orphans restin' or havin' any fun, so she puts 'em to scrubbin' the floor with toothbrushes. Even the ittiest, bittiest orphan, little Sweetness. So one day, Sweetness hit the road.

I found out right away because Mrs. Sump came bustin'
into Loopy Lil's Saloon, hollerin' like a banshee.

"Sheriff!" she yelled (that's me). "That provokin' little
twerp — I mean that dear child, Sweetness, done escaped —
I mean, disappeared! And I'm fit to be tied, worryin' about
that pore thang all pink and helpless, wanderin' lost on the
plains and steppin' on scorpions and fallin' into holes and
such. You gotta bring her back alive — er, I mean, *safe* — before
she runs into *Coyote Pete!*"

That did it. Scorpions were one thing. But Coyote Pete is
as mean as an acre of rattlesnakes, and the toughest, ugliest
desperado in the West.

So I got my star and I buckled on my gun belt and headed west. It was hot as blazes. Seemed like the wind was too tired to blow. Then it got hotter. Hours passed, and what with the sun beatin' down on me, I commenced to feel thirsty. That was when I realized that it woulda been prudent to bring along some water. After some more hours, I begun to stagger with the thirst, and the next thing I knowed, I was plopped down in the dirt. Fortunately, I was in the shade of a big cactus, so I decided to stay there for a spell to catch my breath.

Next thing I knew, I felt this cool, delicious water tricklin'
over my tongue. I popped open my eyes, and there, just a shadow
against the sun, was little Sweetness and her big canteen!

As soon as I was watered up enough to make words come out of my mouth, I said, "Why, Sweetness, thank heaven I've saved you!" And she said, "Yes, sir. Thank you."

That little orphan is just as cute as a speckled pup under a wagon!

"Now I've come to take you home," says I.

"I don't want to go home," says she. "I'm tired of scrubbin' floors with a toothbrush."

"What can't be cured must be endured," I told her. Now, I thought this was very wise advice, but the orphan didn't seem to think so, 'cause she lit off like she was tryin' to catch yesterday.

This day was goin' from bad to worse. Now I was goin' to have to save that orphan again! Also, if you know anythin' about the desert, you know that when the sun goes down in all its glory, it starts to cool off, and then it gets right cold. Also, the snakes come out. So I headed off after Sweetness, all shiverin' and wishin' I'd brought a blanket.

I got to feelin' a trifle hungry, too. Seems like I was
wanderin' around among the snakes and the rocks for a
coon's age, till I was so tuckered out I just curled up against
a bush and went to sleep. Pretty soon I commenced to
dream that I was home with my own dear mama, sittin'
'round the fire all toasty warm and she was cookin' somethin'
nice. Then I woke up and there was the orphan and a camp-
fire, and that little tyke was a-toastin' marshmallows.

"Want one?" says she. Well, doesn't that just beat all?

"Now looky here, Sweetness," I says to her while I was gobblin' down them marshmallows, "this is the second time I done saved you, and I'd very much appreciate it if you'd *stay* saved. So we're gonna mosey on back to that there orphanage right now."

Well, I'll be darned if she didn't start to cry!

"Don't you like me?" she asked.

"Why, sure I do, honey! Ain't I saved you twice? There's nothin' to cry about."

But she went right on bawlin'. "I ain't got no ma," says she. "I ain't got no pa. All I got is Mrs. Sump and a toothbrush."

"Well, ain't no way to fix that lessen you gits adopted," I explained.

Then she smiled up in my face like she was expectin' me to say somethin' particular. It was too deep fer me.

"It sure is a dilemma," was all I could come up with to
say. At which she threw up her little hands in the air an
stomps off into the night.

"Dang!" says I. "Now you quit that! You really fry m
patience." But I was gonna bring that orphan back if it

So there was the sun rising over
the plains, and there I was, feelin' like
somethin' that was chewed up and spit
out, tryin' to find one little orphan out
in the big, wild West.

Now here comes the excitin' part. I had gone fur enough
to work up a good sweat, so I ambled over to a big rock so's
I could stand in the shade. That's when I heard the sound.
Just a little click, like a gun bein' cocked. I turned around
and what'd I see but Coyote Pete, loaded for bear and givin'
me a look that would freeze a cat. I had ta think fast.

"Coyote Pete," I told him, "you can see by the star on my chest that I is here to uphold the law. Now you can't go around shootin' folks and scarin' orphans, and I's here to arrest you."

Now it don't seem like he heard what I said, 'cause just as cool as you please he aimed his six-shooter right at my big silver star.

"Listen here, hamster brain," I says, "you're ridin' for a fall. You put down that there gun or I'm gonna knock you into the middle of next week. I'm gonna snatch you bald-headed. I'm gonna lock you up and throw away the key!"

And you know what he done? He made a sound like "thunk" and fell over backwards, laid out cold like a sacka feed. I scared him that bad! And who should show up just then but Sweetness. She took off her hair ribbons and we tied that varmint up bulletproof and pig tight.

"Now Sweetness," I told her, "I
ain't havin' no more of this runnin'
away. You can't go roamin' around
this here prairie with outlaws all over
the place. It's too dangerous. How
many times has I gotta save you?"

"If you was as smart as you is brave, you could figure out how to save me fer good," she said, lookin' me right in the eye. There we stood, havin' a kinda starin' contest.

"What you leadin' up to?" says I.

"Think," says she.

So I chewed on it awhile longer. "Do it have somethin' to do with adoptin'?"

"You're gettin' it," she says.

I was startin' to get a kinda pretty picture up in my head regardin' me and little Sweetness and a couple a rockin' chairs by the fire.

"Well, sweet child," I says to her, "I knows I's a rough character, but if you was to agree to it, *I* could adopt you."

"Pa!" says she, and she fell on me like Grandma on a chicken snake.

Then me and Sweetness rolled that
varmint all the way back to town.

Now here come the endin'. That very day I done signed them adoption papers.

Then that precious child told me about the seven other orphans and how their toothbrushes was worn down to little nubs with all that scrubbin'. So I adopted them, too.

As for Coyote Pete, we put him in jail and I got a big reward fer bringin' that varmint to justice. After a few years they let him out and put him in the custody of a parole officer. This was none other than Mrs. Sump, who, as you can see, was out of the orphan business. And I don't know how she done it, but she got that desperado to marry her, and now all he does is scrub that floor. And I can tell you, he jumps when she hollers frog.

And that's the truth.

APR 10 2018

NO LONGER PROPERTY OF
SEATTLE PUBLIC LIBRARY